for Mum and Dad

HODDER CHILDREN'S BOOKS

First published in Great Britain in 2019 by Hodder and Stoughton

Text and illustrations copyright © Ellie Sandall 2019

The moral rights of the author and illustrator have been asserted.

A CIP catalogue record of this book
is available from the British Library.

HB ISBN: 978 1 444 93386 4

PB ISBN: 978 1 444 93387 1

10 9 8 7 6 5 4 3 2 1

Printed and bound in China

MIX
Paper from
responsible sources
FSC® C104740
FSC
www.fsc.org

Hodder Children's Books
An imprint of
Hachette Children's Group
Part of Hodder and Stoughton
Carmelite House
50 Victoria Embankment
London, EC4Y 0DZ

An Hachette UK Company
www.hachette.co.uk

www.hachettechildrens.co.uk

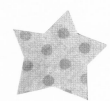

Zzz...

Ellie ☆ Sandall

EVERYBUNNY
Dream!

Zzz...

Zzz...

Hodder Children's Books

Little bunnies like to play.
They have had a busy day.

But now it's late and time to say...

EVERYBUNNY

Bedtime won't be very long.
Time to put pyjamas on.

EVERYBUNNY WASH!

And brush your teeth,

and clean your paws,

and comb your **tail**,

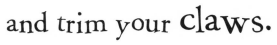

and trim your **claws**.

EVERYBUNNY HUG!

And cuddle up,
    and snuggle tight,
        and close your eyes,

and say goodnight.

But **wait!**
Who's here
in the dark?
A quiet giggle,
muffled bark.

Bunny ears
and bunny socks,

a bushy, orange tail...

A FOX!

A noise outside!
A sudden knock.
Some pointed ears...
Another fox?

And huddle up,
and snuggle in.
A happy smile,
a cheeky grin.

A cosy group,
a peaceful scene.

Every fox cub,

everybunny...

dream.